GRANDFATHER
and I

GRANDFATHER
and I

by
Helen E. Buckley

Pictures by
Paul Galdone

REC ®

LIBRARY EDITION 1970
RESPONSIVE ENVIRONMENTS CORP.
Englewood Cliffs, N.J. 07632

Lothrop, Lee & Shepard Co.　　　*New York*

Eleventh printing, August 1970

Grandfather and I
are going for a walk.
It will be a slow walk

because

Grandfather and I
never hurry.
We walk along
and walk along
And stop…
And look…
just as long
as we like.

Other people we know
are always in a hurry.

Mothers hurry.
They walk in a hurry
and talk in a hurry.
And they always want *you* to hurry.

But Grandfather and I
never hurry.
We walk along
and walk along
And stop…
And look…
just as long as we like.

Fathers hurry.
They hurry
off to work
and they hurry
home again.
They hurry
when they kiss you
and when they
take you for a ride.

But Grandfather and I
never hurry.
We walk along
and walk along
And stop...
And look...
just as long as we like.

Brothers and sisters
hurry, too.
They go so fast
they often bump into you.

And when *they* take you
for a walk
they are always
leaving you far behind.

But Grandfather and I
never hurry.
We walk along
and walk along
And stop…
And look…
just as long as we like.

Things hurry...
Cars and buses,
trains and little boats.
They make noises
when they hurry—

They toot whistles
and blow horns.
And sometimes
scare you.

Grandfather and I never hurry.
We walk along and walk along
And stop...
And look... just as long as we like.

And when Grandfather and I
get home
we sit in a chair
And rock and rock.
And sing a little…
And talk a little…
And rock and rock…
just as long as we like—

Until somebody
tells us to hurry.

Designed and set by Huxley House in 14 pt. Textype.